Family Face-off

D1430901

by Maria Rosado
illustrated by Bob Ostrom

SCHOLASTIC INC.
New York   Toronto   London   Auckland   Sydney
Mexico City   New Delhi   Hong Kong

KLASKY CSUPO, Inc.

Based on the TV series *The Wild Thornberrys*® created by Klasky Csupo, Inc.
as seen on *Nickelodeon*®

ISBN 0-439-22801-8

12 11 10 9 8 7 6 5 4 3 2 1   0 1 2 3 4 5/0

Printed in the U.S.A.   40

First Scholastic printing, October 2000

Chapter 1

Eliza couldn't believe what her father, Nigel, was saying.

"It's true, Marianne," Nigel said. "Darwin's ideas truly are brilliant!"

"Brilliant?" Eliza asked in amazement. She poked her head through the trapdoor in the roof of the Commvee. Nigel and Marianne were steering the multipurpose vehicle through the seas off Ecuador. "You can't really be talking about Darwin?"

"We certainly are, poppet!" Nigel gushed. "Smashing, isn't it? We're going to the Galápagos islands to trace the path of Charles Darwin! The very man who made evolution a household word!"

"Of course!" Eliza said. "THAT Darwin." For a minute, she had thought they were talking about the chimpanzee who lived with the Thornberrys.

Eliza laughed as she told Darwin, the chimp, what had happened. He was also on the roof, and had been scratching himself with his foot.

"They could've been talking about me," Darwin whined.

"Don't get me wrong, Darwin, I know you're brilliant," Eliza whispered to her best friend. "But they can't understand all the intelligent things you say."

"Humph," Darwin snorted.

Thanks to a mysterious shaman, Eliza

could understand Darwin—in fact, she could talk to just about any animal. And it was a secret!

On the horizon, a cluster of tiny lumps was getting larger. Soon they began to look more like islands—The Galápagos Islands. Its volcanic peaks were covered in a fog that drifted away just as the Commvee arrived at Santa Cruz Island.

The Thornberrys headed for the Charles Darwin Research Station to check in with a ranger.

Donnie ran ahead, waving and shouting, "SibeeDARwoowoo!"

Donnie was a half-wild little boy the Thornberrys had found in Borneo. It was hard to understand anything he said. At the station, he tried to climb on the ranger's head.

"Ah, yes, the Thornberrys," the ranger said, as he pried Donnie away. "So happy

to have you back on our islands."

Funny, Eliza thought, he didn't look happy.

"Just remember," the ranger added, "you *must* not bring in any foods or animals which might upset the delicate balance of nature here. No plants, no seeds, and NO pets."

The ranger looked at Darwin.

"Darwin isn't a pet," Eliza protested. "He's a highly valued member of our family."

Darwin picked that moment to scratch his underarm.

"Uh, yes. Well." The ranger sniffed. "How interesting that two famous families would be here at the same time to make the exact same trip."

Nigel's eyes popped open. "What? Who?"

"Leo Léon," said the ranger. "From the show, *Leo Léon, King of the Beasts*."

"Yes, Leo with the ego," Marianne snorted as the ranger walked off.

But Nigel was hopping with excitement. Leo Léon was one of his idols!

"Smashing!" Nigel said, rubbing his hands in glee. "I'd love a chat."

"Who's Leo Léon?" Eliza asked.

Behind them, someone laughed. Eliza whirled around. Then she gasped. She seemed to be looking at a mirror image of her family!

Chapter 2

Except for his yellow hair, Leo could pass as Nigel's twin.

"Silly leetle girl!" Leo sneered. "Only stupid people do not know Leo Léon."

His evil twin, Eliza thought.

Standing beside Leo was his wife, Natasha. She wore a fancy French *chapeau*—otherwise she looked exactly like Marianne. Damien, Leo's teenage son, had wavy blond hair that fell in front of one eye, just like Debbie. There was even someone as wild-looking as Donnie: a very hairy little man wolfing down a chocolate snack.

"That is Marcel, our assistant," Leo said. "And this is Edmond!"

Eliza gasped. A boy, wearing glasses and braces, looked just like her! But, unlike Eliza, he also wore a sneer on his face and a parrot on his shoulder.

"Say 'hi, dweeb-o,' Napoleon," the boy told his parrot.

Nigel began introducing his own family.

"*Oui*. Yes, I know. I have seen your leetle show," Leo said, yawning. "*Seagull Tornbunny's Animal Farm*."

"It's *Nigel Thornberry's Animal World*," Marianne said.

Leo simply shrugged. "Whatever you say. Now, *moi* says that the Léons are here, so the Tornbunnys must go."

Nigel's jaw dropped. He was sure he must have heard wrong. "Er, I say, there's room for both of us! In fact, you're welcome to join us aboard the Commvee. We could join forces, you know!"

Leo looked down his enormous nose at the Commvee. "Pooh! Your leetle car is no good for such a trip."

Then he pointed toward the dock. "*Voila* . . . the Cleopatra!"

Nigel's mustache drooped at the sight of the Léons' vehicle. The Cleopatra looked like the perfect ship for someone as grand as Leo Léon. Suddenly Nigel felt that he and the Commvee were a little shabby.

Damien spoke up. "We have a remote locator system that can spot the smallest bug on the islands. Plus we can put out live TV coverage of our trip twenty-four hours a day!"

"*Oui,* that is right!" Leo said. "We broadcast all over the world."

Nigel's spirits sank more. How could anyone compete with that?

Marianne was worried, too. "Nigel, we've visited the islands before. Maybe we should just leave it to the Léons this time."

Leo laughed. "I knew you would not be able to keep up. Here, it is the 'survival of the fittest,' as Charles Darwin said."

"He didn't say that," Eliza said. She'd been reading about the scientist. "That was some other guy."

Leo pretended not to hear. "The one who will do *anything* to survive is always the winner!"

Eliza didn't agree. Neither did Marianne. "Nigel, I've changed my mind!" she said. "We *are* going to make this trip. We'll prove our way is just as good as his, and . . . well . . . much nicer!"

The Léons looked bored.

"Not only that, we'll do it *faster*," Marianne boldly added.

Suddenly Leo perked up. A race! He listened as Marianne suggested some rules: Both families must visit the four islands Darwin had. They had to spot every one of the animals Darwin had seen and get the proof on film. The first one to return with proof of all the species wins.

"All the species that still exist, that is," Marianne finished.

Leo nodded eagerly. "The whole world will be watching."

Nigel gulped. But Marianne called out after Leo as he and his family walked away. "You're on! And may the best family win!"

Chapter 3

Eliza was about to follow her parents back toward the Commvee when she heard a loud *CRACK!*

It was Edmond, the boy with the parrot. He had just smashed a walnut shell under his heel.

"Caw-haw! Napoleon wants a walnut!" his parrot sang. It gobbled up the nut.

Eliza warned Edmond, "Be careful. You're not allowed to bring seeds to the

Galápagos," she said. "It might mess up the whole food chain. And you could be kicked off the islands!"

Edmond looked thoughtful. "Thanks for the info!" he said, before dropping the walnuts into his pocket and walking away.

A minute later, from out of nowhere, Napoleon swooped down on Eliza and she fell. Edmond helped her up and dusted the sand off her clothes.

"I'm soooooo sorry!" he said. "I don't know what got into Napoleon."

Edmond seemed so kind and helpful, but Eliza thought she heard him snicker as he rushed off to the Cleopatra.

Not long after, the high-tech ship set sail. The Thornberrys were still busy loading supplies onto the Commvee.

Another rule of the race was that both families had to carry all they needed, just as Darwin's ship, the *Beagle*, did. If they ran out of anything, they'd have to go back to Santa Cruz Island to stock up.

"Debbie, please check the water supply," Marianne said. "Eliza, see what that ranger wants."

The ranger was marching up to the Commvee. He wanted to see Eliza.

"Young lady, I received a report that you're carrying seeds onto the islands!" said the ranger angrily. "Will you please empty your pockets?"

Eliza reached into her pockets—and pulled out a handful of walnuts!

"These aren't mine!" she shouted.

Ignoring Eliza, the ranger told Nigel and Marianne that the caller had warned that more nuts were hidden on board the Commvee. He needed to search the whole vehicle.

Eliza was furious! She was sure

Edmond had something to do with this. Even worse, the ranger now wanted the Thornberrys out of the race!

"After all, you broke the rules," he told Eliza.

"But I didn't put them there!"

"Can you prove they came from someplace else?" asked the ranger.

Eliza stomped off while the ranger finished his search. She watched a hawk fly down near the Cleopatra.

"Hawww, hawww! Greedy parrot," Eliza heard the hawk grumble. "All he left is shells, shells, shells!"

Eliza raced back to the Commvee and told the ranger to check the Cleopatra's dock.

Sure enough, a small pile of walnut shells was right on the dock. And everyone saw the bright green parrot feather on top of the shells.

"Ahem!" The ranger huffed. "All right, you may go."

Eliza was excited. "Come on," she shouted to her family. "The Léons have a head start, but we're still in the race!"

Chapter 4

Nigel used the Commvee's top speed to catch up with the Cleopatra. Even so, when they reached their first stop, San Cristóbal Island, it was already night. Visitors weren't allowed into wild areas after dark, so the Thornberrys had to wait until the next day to look for animals.

In the morning, Eliza could hardly wait to explore. She looked toward Cerro

Brujo, a hill formed by the crumbling cone of an old volcano.

"You know, Deb," she said to her sister, "some of the tortoises here are over a hundred years old. Maybe they met Darwin."

"Do I look like I care?" Debbie asked, wiggling her toes. "Hey, Donnie, what do you think?"

"Urrrgggg," Donnie grinned. He had painted stripes on his belly with Debbie's nail polish. Then he aimed the brush at Darwin's nose.

"Ah-hoo-hoo-hoo!" Darwin yelled, running around the roof with his arms in the air.

"What's the hubbub?" asked Nigel, popping up to the roof. "No time for that, pets, we must go ashore!"

Debbie pointed to her freshly painted toenails. "I've got to stay here to let these babies dry. Don't worry, I'll keep Donnie by me."

Eliza grabbed a red notebook from her desk. "I wrote down all the things we have to find in this notebook," she told Darwin. "Charles Darwin carried one just like it."

That afternoon, just as Debbie was painting her fingernails for the fifth time, Damien Léon appeared.

"I can't believe my luck finding you alone!" he said to Debbie. "Want to go to Kicker Rock? It's not far and we might see blue-footed boobies."

Debbie didn't care about birds, but she didn't want Damien to know that. "Uh, sure," she said. "C'mon, Donnie."

Damien frowned. "*No* baby-sitting," he said.

Debbie wouldn't leave Donnie behind. So Damien finally agreed to let Donnie come. But as soon as they were out in the bay, Damien tipped the boat into a wave.

Donnie went flying and landed in the water!

"Wait! Go back!" Debbie screamed.

Damien just sped up. "Forget it. The little runt's probably home by now," he said. "If we go back for him, we'll never reach Kicker Rock before sunset."

Debbie argued, but Damien kept steering out to sea. In the meantime, Donnie had swum back to the Commvee. He howled and shook his dripping fists at the boat as it roared out of sight.

Hours later, Eliza was heading back to the Commvee with Darwin and her parents. They'd found many animals on the small island after a hard climb to the highlands above the bay.

Eliza lagged behind to chat with a giant tortoise. Suddenly she heard her mother call out, "Eliiiiiizaaaa!" Eliza ran back to the Commvee to find her parents pacing in the sand. "Your sister's missing!"

Chapter 5

"Daaaalabaruck. NOgodoneee."

Nigel and Marianne were trying to figure out what Donnie was saying—and keep away from his feet. He kept trying to kick them.

Just then they saw the Léons set sail for the next stop.

Eliza was mad. "Now we'll never win!"

"Eliza! The race isn't important right now," Marianne said. "We have to find Debbie!"

"I know," Eliza said. "It's just not fair, that's all."

Nigel and Marianne went to get flashlights. As Eliza watched the sun begin to sink, she thought about Debbie being alone somewhere. All of a sudden the race didn't seem all that important to Eliza either.

"Let me help look!" she cried.

Nigel placed his hand on her shoulder. "Now, poppet, we don't want both of you getting lost. Wait right here and let us know by radio when she gets back."

He and Marianne hurried off along the beach. Eliza waited exactly one minute. "We have to do something!" she told Darwin.

"KICKeriibbiiii!" Donnie howled. He aimed a kick at Darwin that made the chimp run around in circles.

Eliza suddenly understood. "Debbie's at Kicker Rock!"

She grabbed her flashlight. "Come on,

Darwin!" Eliza called as she started tugging the Thornberrys' motorboat toward the water.

"Don't you think we should wait for your parents? Someone's got to stay on the radio—"

"No time—it's getting dark," Eliza said, starting up the motor. Moaning, Darwin climbed in too. Donnie jumped in right after him.

Soon they were buzzing by the two stony pieces that made up Kicker Rock. A big wave tossed their boat up and down. "I knew this was a bad idea!" Darwin yelled.

"Relax, Darwin, I know what I'm doing," Eliza said. But the truth was Eliza was scared, too. The rising tide was pulling the boat closer to the jagged edges of Kicker Rock. And it was getting too dark to see.

Suddenly she heard a shout. "Eliza! Over here!"

It was Debbie! Eliza steered the boat toward her sister, who was clinging to a ledge, trying to keep above the waves.

"Daaalabruck!" Donnie shouted.

"Are you okay?" Eliza called out.

"OKAY? Are you crazy?" Debbie spit out salt water and swam toward the boat. "Look at my hair!"

Darwin helped Eliza pull her water-logged sister over the side of the boat.

"What happened?" Eliza asked.

"Thanks to that toad, Damien, I almost drowned!" Debbie spluttered. "He told me to climb onto a ledge to get some dumb boobie feather. Then he took off! The tide came up so I got stuck here."

When the girls got back, Nigel and Marianne were frantic.

"Heavens," Nigel said, mopping his brow when he heard their story. "What a narrow escape!" Eliza could tell he was upset at the idea that his idol might stoop to sabotage.

"I'm sure it was just a misunderstanding," Nigel said. "Leo Léon would never do such a thing."

Marianne didn't agree. "*You* wouldn't, Nigel, but Leo isn't as great as you think."

"He's tip-top in his field," Nigel argued, "the absolute *crème de la crème*."

"He's no *crème*, Nigel, he's a crumb," Marianne said. "You're more tip-top than he is, and it's time you realized it."

"Mom's right," Eliza chimed in.

Nigel blushed the color of a red-hot chili pepper. Then he proudly twirled his moustache. "Well, er, if that's what you think . . . there's only one thing to do."

"What's that, Dad?" Debbie asked.

"Prove the Thornberrys are better, pumpkin . . . win this race!"

Chapter 6

Nigel steered the Commvee full steam ahead to Floreana Island. At sunup, they started on their checklist. Their trail began on a beach covered in green sand.

"This is some wacky sand," Debbie said, scooping up a handful. "Maybe I'll paint my toenails this color next time."

"Forget about your toes for a minute, Debbie," Eliza said, holding up a picture of a small drab-looking bird, "and help us look for this finch."

Debbie shrugged. "Why don't we just take its picture on some other island? Damien said finches are all over the Galápagos."

"The medium tree finch lives only on Floreana Island, pet," Nigel explained. He started telling her all about the thirteen different kinds of finches Darwin had found, but Debbie's eyes quickly glazed over.

"Just remember," Eliza said, "if we don't find a medium tree finch here, we don't win."

They headed off into the hills near a lagoon, collecting shots of some flamingos and other birds along the way. Eliza shivered as she looked at the twisted, dead-looking branches of the palo santo trees nearby. They reminded her of the creepy tales she had read about mysterious disappearances on this lonely island.

By the end of the day, the Thornberrys had spotted every animal on their list for the island, except the finch. It seemed to have disappeared as well.

While the Thornberrys took a break at the dock, the Léons returned. Eliza half wished they would vanish off Floreana Island, too, as the family piled aboard the Cleopatra and set off for the next stop.

"I guess that means they found the finch," Marianne sighed. "It's getting late. If we don't see one soon, we'll be here another day."

"Oh, I know what will cheer everyone up," Nigel said. He stepped into the Commvee and came out carrying a big plate.

"Uh-oh," Eliza groaned.

"Look, everyone! Kippers!" Nigel called out, smiling happily.

The second the plate hit the picnic table, Donnie moved in.

"Now, lad, leave a few for us," Nigel said. "I'm sure we'd all like some."

Donnie started flinging the fish around.

"Look out!" Eliza yelled.

"Incoming!" Debbie hollered. They both ducked under the table.

The next kipper hit Darwin—*SMACK!*—on the nose. He howled. "Ah-oo-ee-ee!"

Darwin ran around with his hands over his face, right into a tree! "Yowwww!"

The chimpanzee whimpered as he lay on the ground. Some leaves and a little brown blob dropped out of the tree and onto his belly.

"Are you okay?" Eliza ran over.

"No, I most certainly am not! That kipper smarted. And it stinks!" Darwin whined.

"I didn't mean you, Darwin," Eliza said. She gently picked up the small blob. The

blob ruffled its feathers and two bright eyes emerged.

"Say, how'd you know my name is Darwin?" the bird asked.

Eliza grinned. They were following the path of Charles Darwin with a chimp named Darwin. Now this bird had the same name, too?

"Your name is Darwin?" she asked the bird.

"All us finches here are named after Darwin, who noticed our very beautiful beaks," the bird said, showing off its own.

"Hey, you're a medium tree finch, aren't you?" Eliza asked. "Would you mind if we took your picture?"

As it turned out, there was nothing the bird would have liked more.

Soon Marianne was filming the finch as it sat on a branch. "Why, it's almost as if he's posing," she marveled.

Chapter 7

With every species on Floreana Island accounted for, the Thornberrys set off for Isabela Island. There, the easiest animals to spot were the sea iguanas Charles Darwin had called "alligators in miniature." They swam right by the Commvee.

It was hot and dusty. When the Thornberrys found all the animals on the island, they returned to the Commvee.

Eliza spotted the Léons' parrot staggering around their vehicle.

"What's that mangy bird doing here?" Darwin asked Eliza.

"Dizzy!" Eliza heard the bird mutter. "Oooh . . . my aching head."

Eliza noticed that Napoleon's beak was covered with scratches. But before she could help him, the parrot took off. He zigzagged toward the Cleopatra, which set sail soon after he landed.

Marianne and Eliza shrugged their shoulders. Debbie climbed into the Commvee for a drink. A second later she was back.

"Hey, what's up with the water?" asked Debbie.

"Why? What's wrong with it?" Marianne asked in reply.

"Nothing, that's what," Debbie said. She held up an empty glass. Everyone piled inside. They tried every sink and shower in the Commvee. No water anywhere.

Then they went outside to check the tanks. They all gasped. The tanks were pitted with holes!

"How could this happen?" Marianne asked.

"It's the Léons!" Eliza said. "Edmond must've made his bird poke holes in the tanks!"

"Now, Eliza," Nigel said. "You can't just go around accusing people without proof."

He simply could not imagine Leo Léon trying to win the race by trickery. Then Eliza spotted bird tracks and what looked to be a boy's footprints in the wet sand below the tanks.

Nigel sighed and shook his head. He finally accepted that his idol Leo would do anything to win. "Well," Nigel said. "I

certainly won't trust that chap again."

"About time," Debbie muttered.

"Don't be rude to your father," Marianne snapped. "Even if he should have known Leo was a louse."

"Marianne!" Nigel huffed.

Pretty soon they all were arguing. Even Donnie seemed upset. He was running around in circles and hooting. "FooooOG Hadadada. FooooOG."

"Now look what you've done!" Nigel scolded. "That may look like the Tibetan fog-calling dance but I'm sure it's just the lad's way of showing he's upset."

Worse yet, the race rules said they had to return to Santa Cruz for more water. By the time they reached the research station, no one was talking to anyone else, except for Eliza and Darwin.

"We'll never win now," Eliza said to Darwin. The two of them were walking through the station while the tanks were being fixed. "Not with everyone fighting. And not if those sneaky Léons keep cheating."

They walked by a huge tortoise sitting in the sun. Eliza read the sign in front of its pen.

"This is so sad, Darwin," she said. "He's called Lonesome George because he's the last of his kind."

"What do you mean? We've seen lots of giant turtles," Darwin said.

"There are all different kinds. George is the very last one just like him."

"It's terrible being the only one of your kind," said the tortoise. He had moved slowly closer to Eliza and Darwin.

Eliza introduced herself and Darwin. "We're here with my family."

"Family." George sighed. "What a wonderful word."

"I guess," sighed Eliza. "Although sometimes it isn't always easy being in one."

"You never know what it means to be part of a family until you don't have one anymore," George said sadly. "I might not be in this mess if my family had just learned to adapt. We liked living spread out all over our island. If we had stuck together instead, we might have been able to save the family."

Eliza nodded. "George, you're absolutely right. And there's something I've got to do—right now!"

Chapter 8

"We all have to get along!"

Marianne looked up from the water tank when Eliza came running up.

"Eliza, honey, I'm glad you're back. I'm sorry I acted so grumpy before."

Nigel popped his head out of a window. "Likewise, luvs. I think we were in a bit of a kerfluffle. But all's cheery now, arr-arr!" He came out to give them all a big hug.

Eliza said. "If we're ever going to beat

the Léons, we're going to have to stick together—as a family."

"Well, duh!" said Debbie. "But we don't stand a chance unless something happens to the Léons. Like getting lost at sea."

"How about a little fog instead?" Nigel asked with a toothy grin.

He explained that he had just heard the weather report. The famous Galápagos fog was rolling in—the worst anyone had seen in years.

"Fog? Like the kind you get when you do a Tibetan fog-calling dance?" Eliza asked. Everyone turned to stare at Donnie, who had his toes in his mouth.

"Well, their ship looks like it can find its way through anything," Debbie grumbled.

"Don't fret, poodles," said Nigel. "A beastly fog can work wonders on high-tech motors, too." He looked at them. "What do you say we give it a go, eh?"

Marianne raced for the driver's seat. Debbie closed all the hatches. Eliza and Darwin sat by the radio, listening for more weather reports.

Nigel muttered something about "that kipper thingee" and disappeared below with a wrench.

The Commvee raced on. They didn't see the fog until it surrounded them like a giant cloud. Soon everything on board was dripping.

Suddenly Eliza yelled, "Guess what I just heard on the radio? The Léons have lost power! They haven't even made it to Santiago Island yet!"

"Hooray!" Marianne, Debbie, and Eliza shouted.

The Commvee's motor purred on for a while. When their locator became too wet to work, Marianne's expert map-reading led them right to Santiago.

The Thornberrys landed on the island at dawn. They climbed out of the Commvee just as the Cleopatra sailed in.

"Quick, pets," Nigel shouted. "We haven't got much of a head start!"

They all took off. Everyone kept an eye out for the animals and plants on Eliza's list.

By midday the list was done. "And it's all thanks to *moi*," said Debbie.

Debbie had spotted the rare land iguana, almost stepping on its tail when she wandered off the trail.

Marianne got a good shot of the shy yellow lizard before it ran away. She also got a good shot of Debbie yelling as she ran the *other* way.

Now it was time to head back to Santa Cruz. The rangers would be waiting to see who arrived first.

"Look, there's the Cleopatra!" Eliza

pointed to the bay. It was just chugging out to sea.

Everyone raced to the Commvee. Soon they were catching up to the Cleopatra, which was moving very slowly. Their ship's motor groaned. There was too much fog water in the fuel.

"They'll never make it!" Eliza shouted.

Just then the Commvee gave a low groan too. And a second later, the motor stopped.

"Looks like *we're* not going to make it, either," said Debbie.

Chapter 9

BRROOM! Brroom! The Commvee started up again with a roar even louder than before. Eliza gasped.

Nigel climbed up from the engineering area. He had a greasy smear on his nose.

"Dad! What did you do?" Eliza asked, giving him a big hug.

Nigel twirled the wrench on one finger. "I told you I was going to give the motor a bit of a fix, what? I hooked it up to a new source of power: waterproof gasoline made of kipper oil!"

"I used up my whole supply," Nigel added sadly. "But there's enough to get to Santa Cruz Island."

The Commvee charged ahead. Soon it was neck and neck with the Cleopatra. Eliza could see Leo glaring at them.

The two ships were almost at the dock, which was crowded with people. Rangers waited with stopwatches.

"We're winning!" Eliza shouted, at the same moment that the Commvee ran out of kipper oil. The Thornberrys stared at each other in dismay as the Commvee drifted to a stop.

"Paddle!" Eliza yelled.

They all climbed down to the Commvee's big floats. Everyone started paddling. But the Cleopatra was gaining. And just as they reached the dock, the Cleopatra pulled ahead.

"Lost by a whisker!" Nigel gasped.

"It isn't over yet!" cried Eliza. She ran inside to get her notebook and Marianne's film. Then they went down to the dock.

"*Voila!* Behold the winner: Leo Léon, King of the Beasts!" Leo was shouting to the crowd. Then he waved at everyone as though he were really some kind of king.

But the ranger held up his hand. "The winner won't be announced until we have checked off all the animals on the lists!" he said.

The rangers went into the station while the Thornberrys and Léons waited outside. Leo started signing autographs— and charging for them.

Eliza and Darwin went to visit Lonesome George. He seemed a lot happier. The rangers had introduced him to a female tortoise from another family.

Finally the ranger came back out. "We checked the lists. We watched the films," the ranger announced. "And the winner is . . ."

Leo Léon began to bow.

"The Thornberrys!"

The crowd cheered.

"WHAT?" Leo roared.

It turned out the Léons had spotted only twelve different kinds of finches. Darwin had counted thirteen.

"You forgot the medium tree finch," the ranger said. "The Thornberrys didn't." He gave Eliza a wink before walking off.

Leo was practically purple with rage. He stormed away with his family, and the Cleopatra took off in a puff of sour black smoke.

"I guess they should have looked up Darwin's finches like you did, squirt," Debbie said, tugging one of Eliza's pigtails.

"If the Léons had spent less time

playing tricks and more time learning what they needed to stay in the race, they would have won," Marianne said.

"No, they wouldn't," said Debbie. She and Marianne burst out laughing. Nigel started to "arr-arr" along with them. Darwin and Donnie joined in.

Eliza got the giggles too. "This is the 'survival of the Thornberrys!'"

Discovery Facts

Blue-footed booby: A bird with sky-blue webbed feet found on many of the Galápagos Islands.

Darwin: Sir Charles Darwin: A naturalist who visited the Galápagos Islands in 1835.

Ecuador: A country in South America.

Finch: A type of bird. Darwin observed thirteen different kinds of finches in the Galápagos.

Floreana Island (also called Santa María): An island in the Galápagos that was named Charles when Darwin visited.

Galápagos Islands: An "archipelago," or group of islands, 600 miles west of Ecuador.

Iguana: A type of large lizard. The sea, or marine, iguana of the Galápagos is the only sea-going lizard in the world. The land iguana is bright yellow.

Isabela Island: The biggest island in the Galápagos; known as Albermarle when Darwin visited.

Kicker Rock: A large rock off the coast of San Cristóbal Island, it's all that remains of the cone of an old volcano.

Lonesome George: A real-life tortoise who lives at the Charles Darwin Research Station. He is the last of the Pinta Island tortoises.

Penguins: Large flightless sea birds. Penguins can live in the Galápagos because of a cold current that passes nearby.

San Cristóbal Island: One of the Galápagos islands; named Chatham at the time of Darwin's visit.

Santa Cruz Island: The site of the Charles Darwin Research Station and the most populated island in the Galápagos.

Santiago Island (also called San Salvador): An island in the Galápagos; it was called James when Darwin visited.

Survival of the Fittest: The theory that only the strongest members of a species will survive and reproduce. Over time, the whole species grows stronger as those traits are passed along.

Tortoise: A turtle-like reptile that can weigh as much as 550 pounds, and live 150 years or longer. Once fourteen kinds of tortoises lived in the Galápagos, now there are just eleven.

Darwin and the Galápagos

In 1831, Charles Darwin set sail from England on the *Beagle*. He was going on a four-year journey around the coasts of South America.

The young scientist was fascinated with the idea of "natural selection," the belief that species of animals and plants can change over time—sometimes becoming a whole different species! Many people did not agree with this idea.

But Darwin's observations of plants and animals on the *Beagle's* visit to the Galápagos Islands helped to change that. He wrote about his findings in the 1859 book, *Origin of Species*. It caused an uproar! For the first time, someone offered proof that the theory of natural selection could be true.

Today scientists still debate Darwin's ideas. And the islands are protected so that modern visitors can have a firsthand look at Darwin's observations.

About the Author

Maria Rosado has written more than a dozen books for young readers, using a number of pen names, as well as stories for *Nickelodeon Magazine* and other publications for children.

She shares a tiny apartment in New York City with her cartoon-loving husband, one cat, and hundreds of books. Maria grew up in New Jersey and when she was younger, she kept a little turtle as a pet—but it escaped. Maria thinks it could have swum off to the Galápagos Islands to commune with the tortoises!